# THE CLUMSY CROCODILE

## Felicity Everett

## Designed by Maria Wheatley and Alex de Wolf

## Illustrated by Alex de Wolf

Language and Reading Consultant: David Wray
Education Department, University of Exeter, England

Series Editor: Gaby Waters

First published in 1994 by Usborne Publishing Ltd, Usborne House, 83-85 Saffron Hill, London EC1N 8RT, England. Copyright © 1994 Usborne Publishing Ltd.

Everglades was no ordinary department store.

It sold things that you just couldn't buy anywhere else.

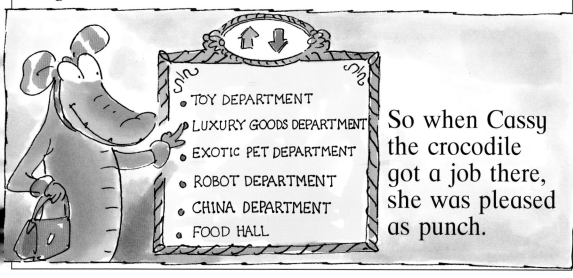

- TOY DEPARTMENT
- LUXURY GOODS DEPARTMENT
- EXOTIC PET DEPARTMENT
- ROBOT DEPARTMENT
- CHINA DEPARTMENT
- FOOD HALL

So when Cassy the crocodile got a job there, she was pleased as punch.

But things didn't go quite
as well as Cassy hoped.

In the china department,
she packed sixty cups
and saucers,

in a bottomless crate.

In the toy department, her tail knocked the Toytown Express off the rails.

In the food hall, she upset the salad.

I'll see you in my office.

And that upset someone very important indeed.

Who was he?

5

The boss shook his head.

The boss sighed.

He told Cassy to go
to the Luxury Goods
department first thing
on Monday morning.

Who were the Greedy Boys?

Cassy was determined to make a fresh start.

All day Sunday she worked on her stacking, wrapping,

and serving with a smile.

Then she put on her Everglades badge and admired herself in the mirror.

CASSY
MAY I
HELP
YOU?

What did the badge say?

On Monday morning,
Cassy was the first to arrive in
the Luxury Goods department.

The security guard was
finishing breakfast.

Now you're here, I'll head for home.

But I don't know what to do!

The guard told her to keep her eye on the Everglades Emerald.

Why was the Everglades Emerald so precious?

Cassy wasn't the only one with her eye on the Everglades Emerald.

What was Nigel worried about?

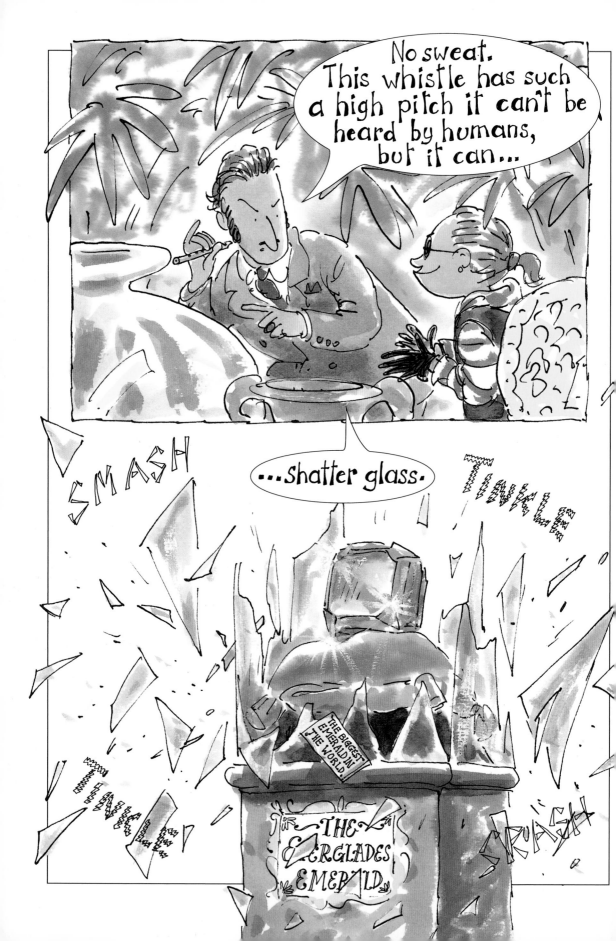

The Greedy Boys didn't realize it,
but Cassy <u>had</u> heard the whistle.
Why?

Cassy thought the whistle sounded like the Toytown Express.

She dashed off to check that no one was messing with the train.

But her tail got caught
on a pearl necklace.

The
pearls
went
everywhere.

And so did
the Greedy Boys.

Which department was Cassy heading for?

Thinking they were customers, Cassy tried to help them up.

But she stumbled on the emerald...

...and crashed into a table.

What was on the table?

But the boss saw the emerald lying on the floor,

and quickly put two and two together.

No need. You've saved the Everglades Emerald and caught the Greedy Boys.

How did he know they were the Greedy Boys?

That afternoon the boss gave a party for Cassy at Everglades.

The whole town was there.

Except for the Greedy Boys. They were safely behind bars.

The Mayor presented Cassy with a special medal.

What did it say?

The next day Cassy went to work at Everglades as usual.

But from now on she could play the latest video games,

eat chocolates and drink pink lemonade.

What was her new job?